DC★SUPER FRIENDS

Green Lantern vs. the Meteor Monster!

By D. R. Shealy

Illustrated by Erik Doescher, Mike DeCarlo, and David Tanguay

A Random House PICTUREBACK® Book
Random House 🏠 New York

DC SUPER FRIENDS and all related titles, characters, and elements are trademarks of DC Comics. Copyright © 2011 DC Comics. All rights reserved. Published in the United States by Random House Children's Books, a division of Random House, Inc., 1745 Broadway, New York, NY 10019, and in Canada by Random House of Canada Limited, Toronto. Pictureback, Random House, and the Random House colophon are registered trademarks of Random House, Inc.
ISBN: 978-0-375-87297-6
www.randomhouse.com/kids
Printed in the United States of America
10 9 8 7 6 5 4 3 2 1

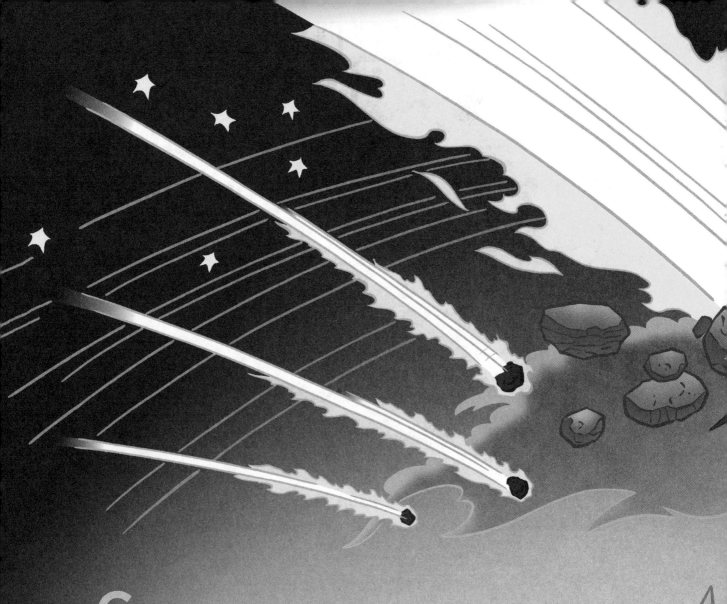

Green Lantern was soaring over the city of Metropolis on his daily patrol of Earth. Suddenly, the sky darkened and flaming meteors began hurtling down from space.

"Those meteors could mean big trouble if they crash into anything!" Green Lantern said.

Green Lantern smashed the closest meteor into a million
tiny pieces by creating a shield with his amazing power ring.

Green Lantern quickly created a large net with his ring. He flew through the sky, scooping up the meteors before they struck the city. But one fiery meteor escaped his net!

There was a sudden flash of red-hot light! Superman had arrived and vaporized the last meteor with his heat vision.

"Good work!" Green Lantern shouted.

"Let's get going," Superman replied. "Batman and Hawkman need us."

Green Lantern and Superman quickly
met up with Hawkman and Batman.
"My radar shows a giant meteor
heading straight for Metropolis," Batman
said over the Batwing's comlink.

Green Lantern produced a long rubber band with his power ring.
Superman grabbed one end, and the two heroes held on with every ounce of
their strength as the meteor slammed into it and stretched it tight. SNAP!
The meteor shot up and away from the city.

The Super Friends dashed to the impact site, where the meteor had landed. They peered into the smoldering crater.

"That meteorite doesn't look like the others," Green Lantern said, generating a force field to protect his friends from the hot space rock.

Superman scanned the meteorite with his X-ray vision and replied,
"That's because it's a—"
"Look out!" Green Lantern shouted.

A giant alien burst out of the crumbling meteorite!
"MMMMAAAAARRRAWWW!" it roared at the Super Friends.
"My power ring can translate alien languages," Green Lantern said.
"Maybe I can talk to this creature."

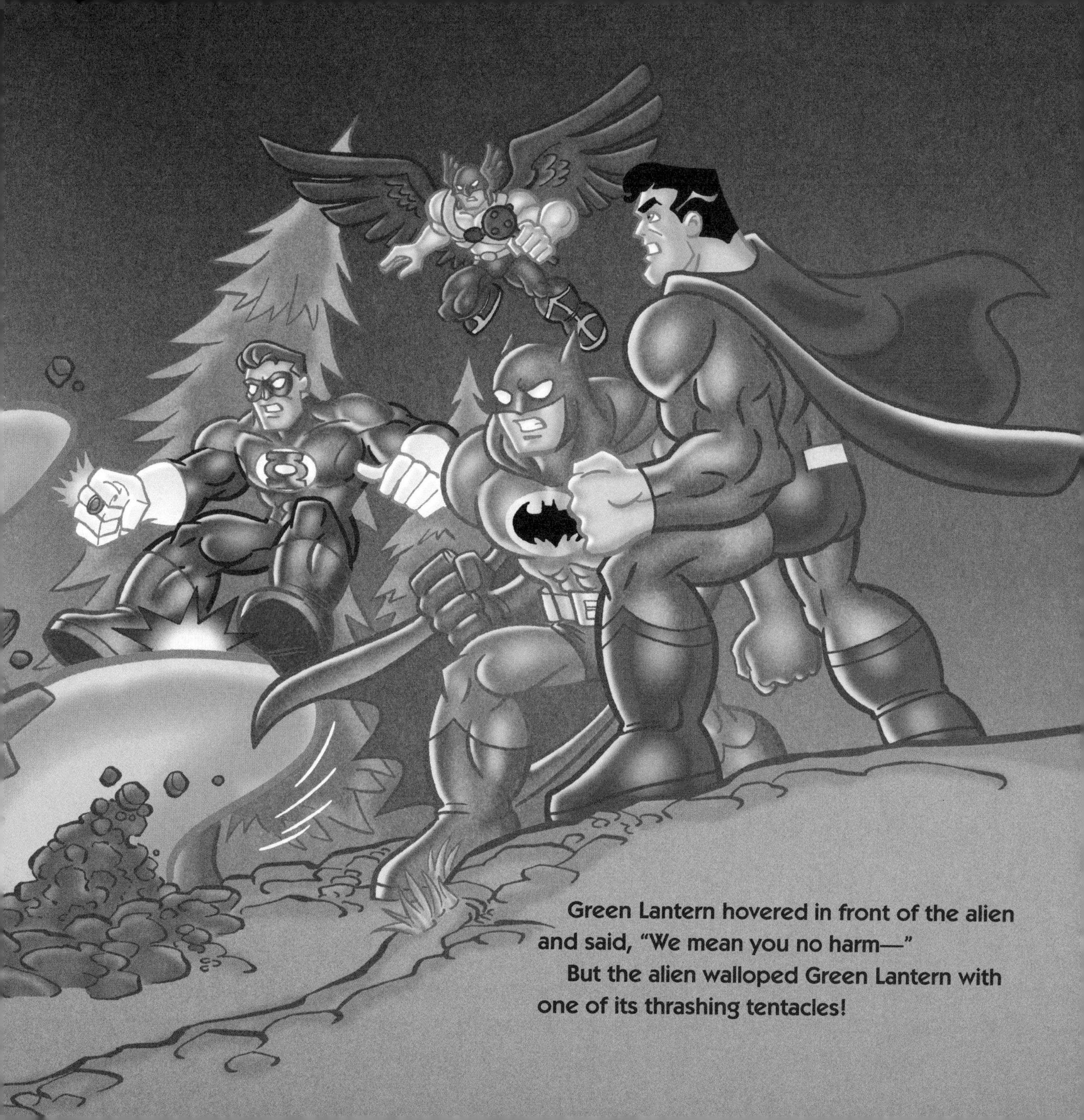

Green Lantern hovered in front of the alien and said, "We mean you no harm—"

But the alien walloped Green Lantern with one of its thrashing tentacles!

The alien crawled out of the crater and headed straight toward the shimmering skyline of Metropolis. It snapped towering trees as if they were twigs and shoved boulders aside as if they were marbles.

"We can't let it reach the city," Batman said. "That meteor monster will destroy everything in its path!"

The Super Friends used all their powers, but the alien could not be stopped. Its skin was harder than rock. Batman's Batarangs bounced off it. Hawkman's mace couldn't dent it. And Superman's heat vision only made the alien angrier!

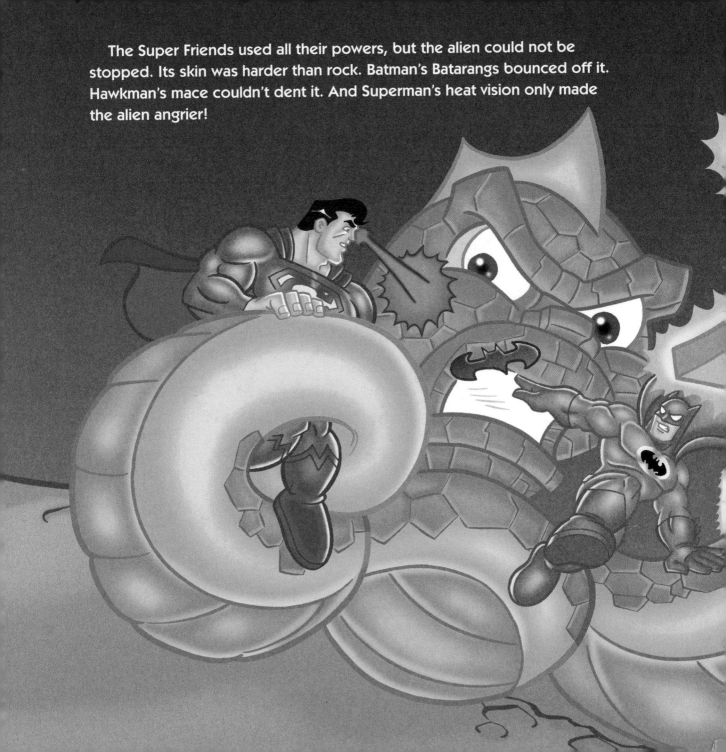

Green Lantern created a giant green bulldozer blade and pushed against the alien with all his might.

"We're not even slowing it down," Green Lantern said.

Suddenly, a dark shadow passed over the Super Friends. They looked up to see two much larger aliens descending from the sky!

"I think our trouble just tripled," Batman said.

"MMMAAAAARRRAWWW!" the small alien howled.

"I've got it!" Green Lantern shouted. "Follow me—I'm going to need everyone's help."

Green Lantern used his power ring to slip a giant fireman's trampoline under the alien. Superman and Hawkman gripped the frame.

"Now lift . . . ," Green Lantern called out, "gently!"

Working together, the Super Friends carried the alien into the sky. It reached toward one of the giant aliens and cooed, "MMMAAAWW-MAAAA!"

As the two aliens reached for the smaller alien, it bounced off the trampoline and right into their arms.

"We didn't mean any harm to your baby," Green Lantern explained through his power ring translator. "It's just that he's a *very* big, um . . . boy."

Green Lantern led the alien family back into space.

"You were on your way to the Omega Centauri galaxy? That meteor storm really *did* throw you off course!" Green Lantern said to the aliens. "Let me show you the way home."

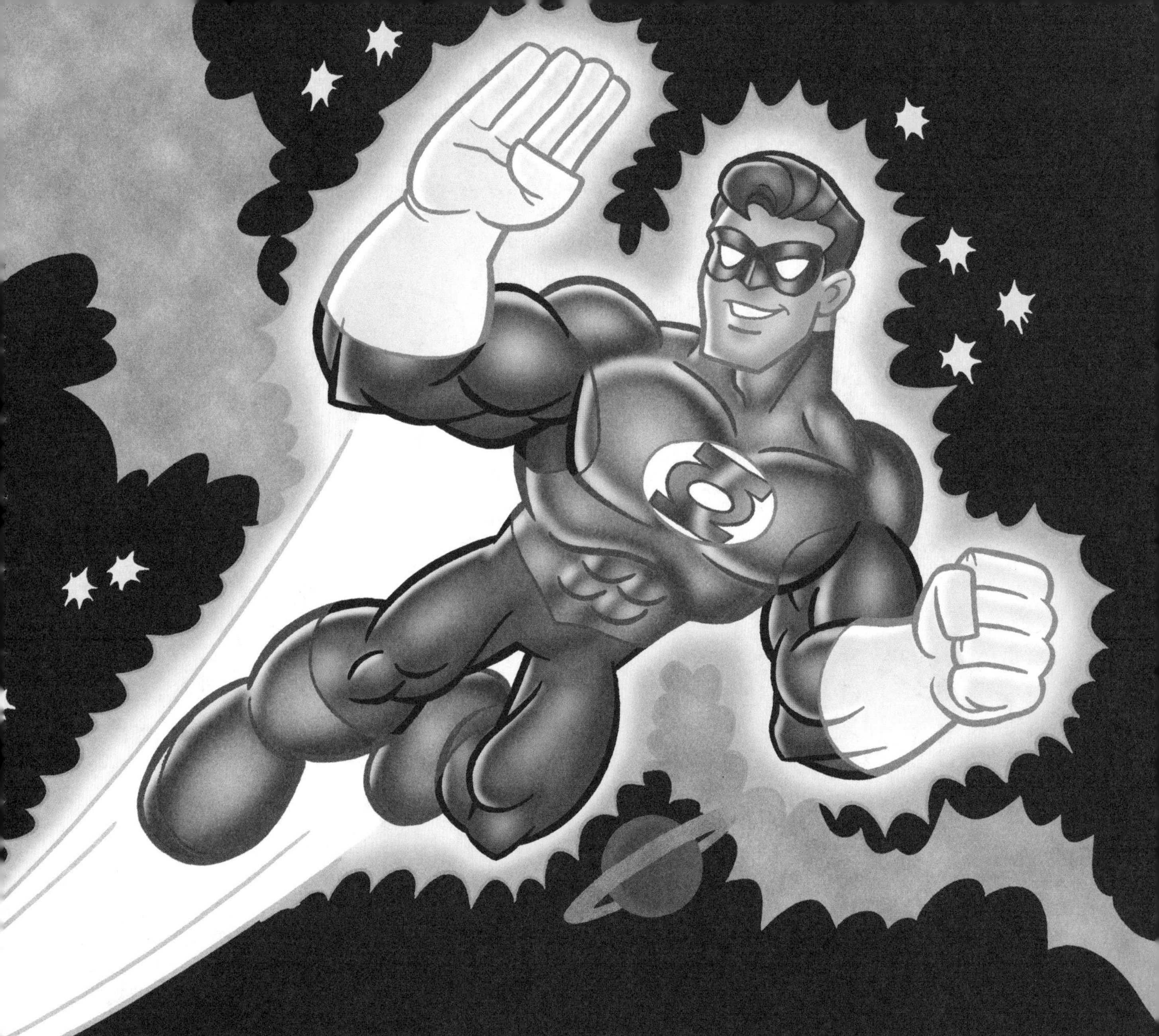

When they reached the edge of the solar system, Green Lantern waved to the aliens and shouted, "Have a safe journey, friends!"

Green Lantern returned to Earth, rocketing through the clear sky. As he rejoined the other Super Friends, Batman said, "There's no time to lose. Joker and Mr. Freeze are taking over Gotham City."

"Let's go," Green Lantern replied. "Anything is better than babysitting!"